A Horse Story

Sami and Thomas meet Pascal

James McDonald

HOUSE OF LORE

A Horse Story
Sami and Thomas meet Pascal

Copyright © 2013 by James McDonald

To the man that missed the bus, be well.

ISBN: 978-0-9886598-4-1

www.HouseofLore.net

First House of Lore paperback edition, 2013

Book Website
www.SamiAndThomas.com

In a cozy country cottage,
With their grandma and her cat,
Sami and Thomas were playing,
A funny game of this and that.

"Can we please go outside Grandma?"
Sami asked with puppy eyes.
"Just one more second Sami,"
Grandma Lamb said to her cries.

"The neighbor's coming over,
And I think that you'll be pleased,
Because he has a favor to ask,
That's sure to keep you busy as bees."

Then before another word was said,
There was a knock upon the door.
And to this day pass, neither lad nor lass,
Could have imagined what was in store.

"Good day to you dear Henry,"
Grandma Lamb said, filled with joy.
"These are the two I've been speaking of,
Sami the girl, and Thomas the boy."

"It's good to meet the both of you.
I hear you're very smart.
Your grandma says you like horses Sami,
From the bottom of your heart."

Sami looked a little timid,
Until her grandma said, "It's okay."
Then all of the sudden she burst out talking,
About riding a horse one day.

"I do love all the horses!"
Said Sami, jumping high.
"And one day I'm going to ride a horse,
While the rolling hills go by."

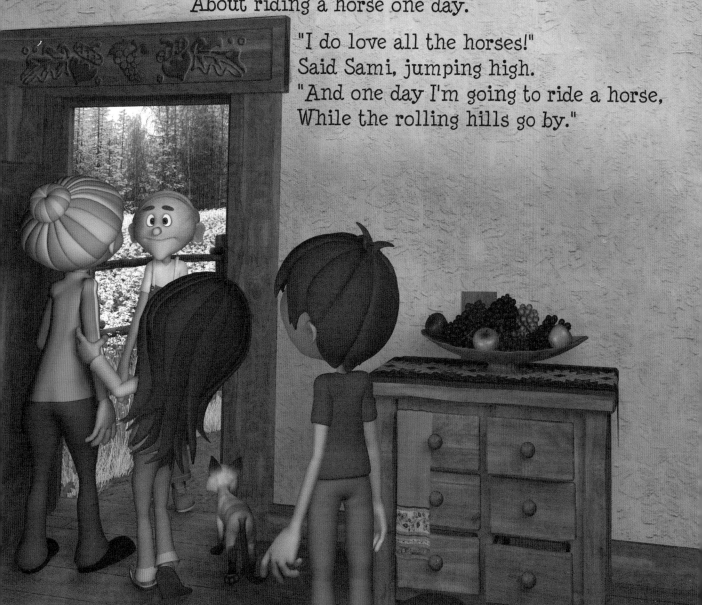

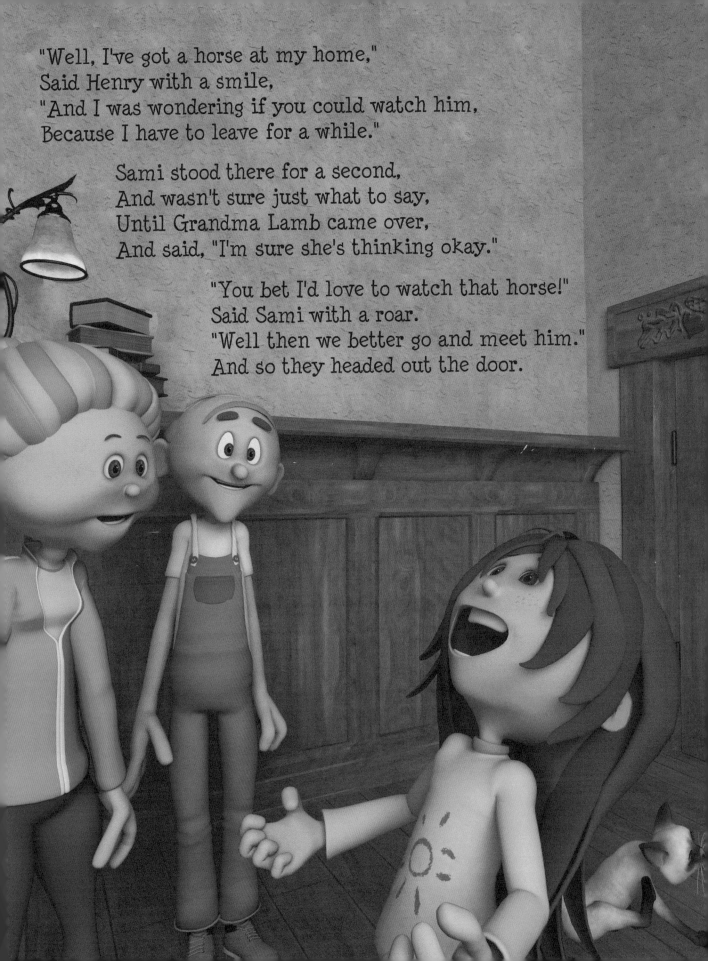

"Well, I've got a horse at my home,"
Said Henry with a smile,
"And I was wondering if you could watch him,
Because I have to leave for a while."

Sami stood there for a second,
And wasn't sure just what to say,
Until Grandma Lamb came over,
And said, "I'm sure she's thinking okay."

"You bet I'd love to watch that horse!"
Said Sami with a roar.
"Well then we better go and meet him."
And so they headed out the door.

It was a beautiful day in the country,
And in the distance was the barn.
Sami could barely control herself,
Like a cat with a ball of yarn.

And there within the shadows,
Was the proud and noble steed,
With his beautiful tail, swishing to and fro,
While chewing on some feed.

"His name's Pascal," said Henry,
"And he's as gentle as they come.
Why if you dipped your hand in sugar,
He might just suck your thumb."

Then all of the sudden ole Henry,
Lifted Sami in the air,
And set her on the horse's back,
To which nothing could compare.

"You can take ahold of Pascal's mane,
And he'll walk you all around."
Sami Lamb was so happy,
She could barely make a sound.

As Pascal walked around the yard,
Sami sat up tall and smiled,
For a friendship was blooming,
Between a horse, and a child.

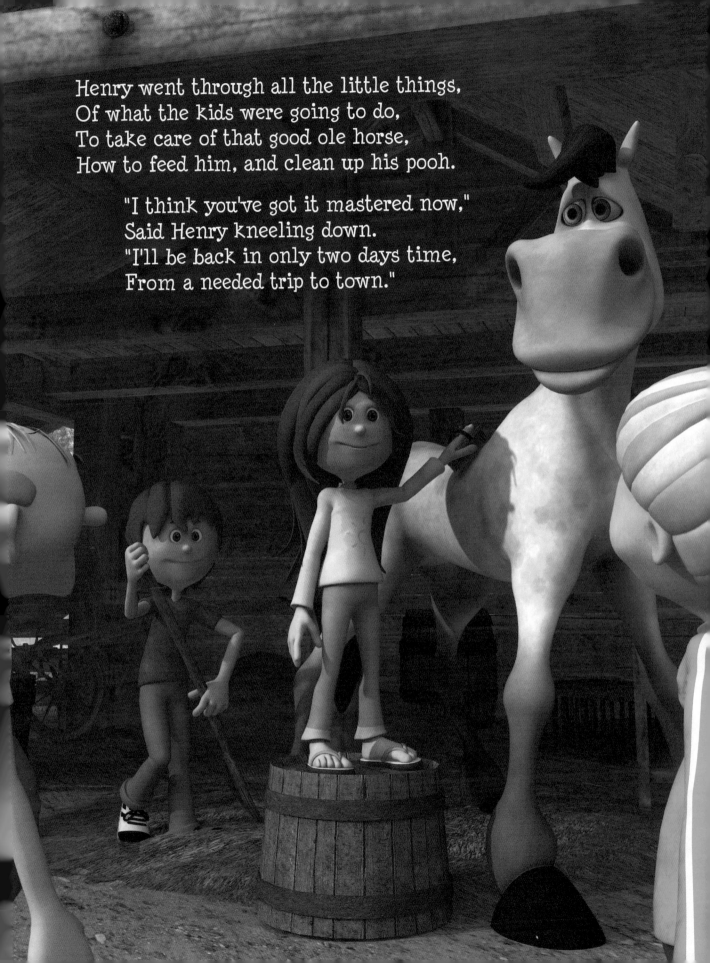

Henry went through all the little things,
Of what the kids were going to do,
To take care of that good ole horse,
How to feed him, and clean up his pooh.

"I think you've got it mastered now,"
Said Henry kneeling down.
"I'll be back in only two days time,
From a needed trip to town."

Then Henry got into his truck,
And headed on his way.
Grandma Lamb hugged both the kids,
And said, "I think we'll call it a day."

That night around the dinner table,
All Sami could do was talk,
About sitting on the horse's back,
And going for a walk.

Then they gathered by the fire,
And read books into the night,
Until both the kids fell fast asleep,
And Grandma Lamb turned out the light.

The next day when the kids woke up,
They headed for the door.
"Now wait a second both of you.
You've got to eat your breakfast before."

"Oh Grandma, can we go real quick,
And say hello to dear Pascal?"
Then Grandma Lamb said, "Really quick,
But stay out of the corral."

So the brother and sister ran super fast,
To say hello to the neighbor's horse,
Then headed home to eat some food,
And set out upon their course.

With Grandma Lamb leading the way,
The kids began to clean.
"Yuck... what is that awful smell?"
Sami Lamb so suddenly screamed.

"If you're going to own a horse Sami,
You've got to clean its stall."
And with those words Sami grabbed the tools,
And the wheelbarrow to haul.

In no time flat the stall was clean,
And the horse had been brushed twice.
"Can I ride him Grandma?" Sami asked.
"Mr. Henry said he's super nice."

"I'm sorry Sami, but the answer's no.
We cannot take a chance.
For you could fall right to the ground,
If the horse reared up or pranced."

"Alright Grandma, that's okay,"
Said Sami as best she could.
So instead they watched the horse all day,
Like good horse-sitters should.

The very next day was exactly the same,
It was horse, horse, horse, and more horse,
And Sami Lamb was caring for Pascal,
As best she should could, of course.

She led her horse friend all around,
And fed him oats and hay.
She brushed his coat so gently,
It was such a fun-filled day.

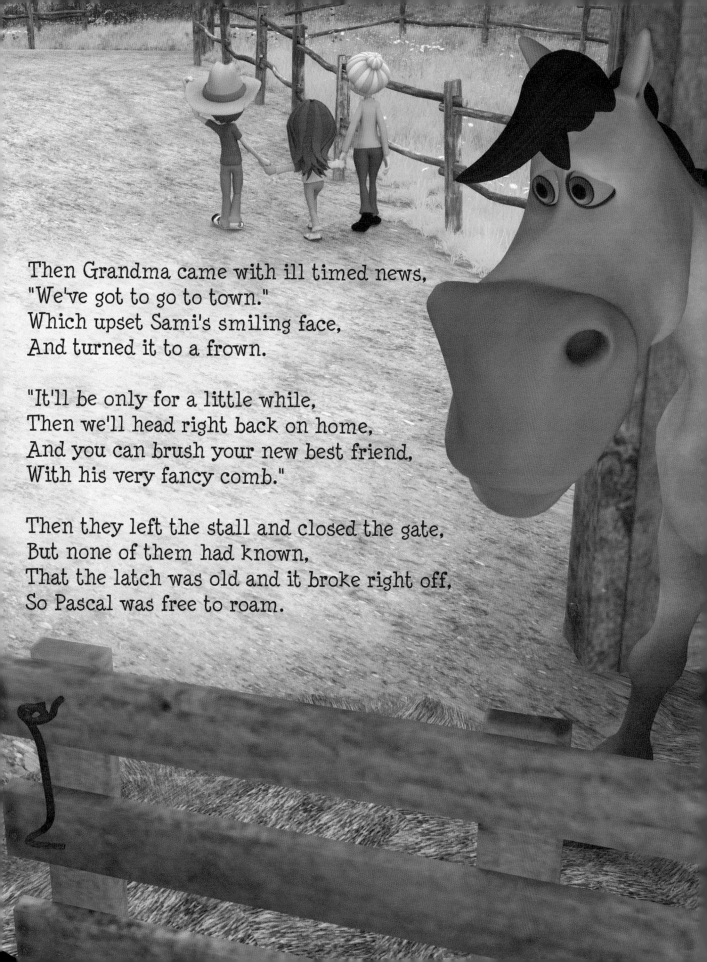

Then Grandma came with ill timed news,
"We've got to go to town."
Which upset Sami's smiling face,
And turned it to a frown.

"It'll be only for a little while,
Then we'll head right back on home,
And you can brush your new best friend,
With his very fancy comb."

Then they left the stall and closed the gate,
But none of them had known,
That the latch was old and it broke right off,
So Pascal was free to roam.

As Grandma Lamb tried to start the car,
It sputtered and it smoked.
"I think this car has seen its day,"
Thomas very gently joked.

With a bang and boom the car revved up,
And they travelled down the trail.
Into Cottage Cove they drove,
At the speed of a very slow snail.

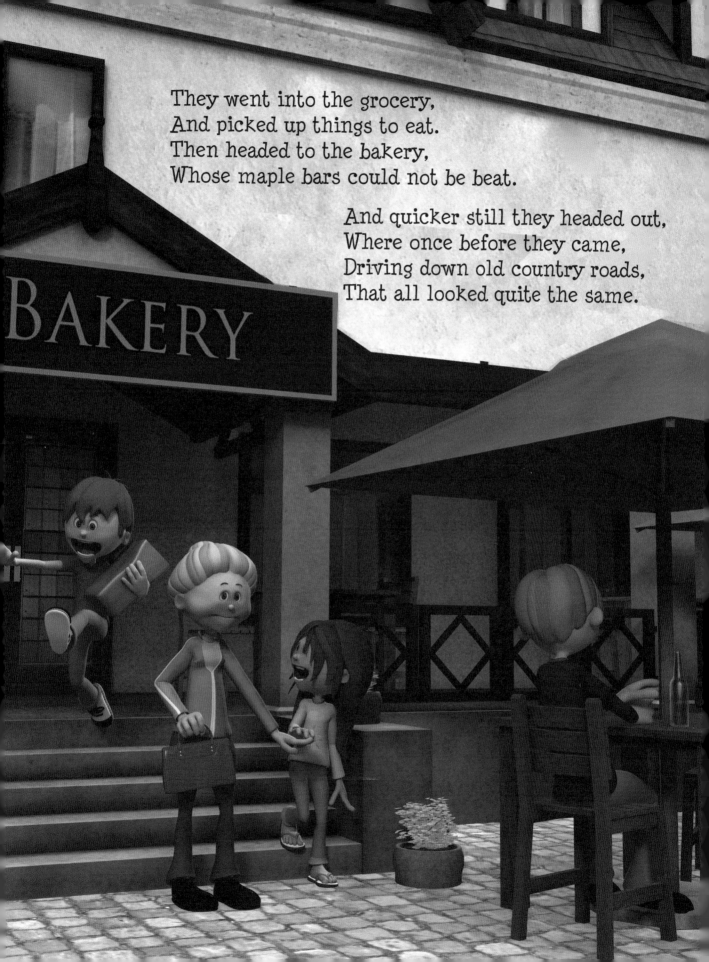

They went into the grocery,
And picked up things to eat.
Then headed to the bakery,
Whose maple bars could not be beat.

And quicker still they headed out,
Where once before they came,
Driving down old country roads,
That all looked quite the same.

BAKERY

When they arrived they gasped with shock,
To see the open gate,
With not one sign of poor Pascal,
And no one knowing of his state.

"You kids go out and look around,
I've got to make a call,
And tell Henry that his horse is free,
Because the lock broke off the stall."

So the kids went out to the open field,
Where flowers bloom about.
"Pascal where are you my best friend!"
Is what Sami Lamb would shout.

"I hope we find him brother dear,"
Said Sami looking sad.
"I know we will," Thomas said to her,
In hopes that she'd be glad.

They came upon a fun-filled pond,
That beckoned them to play,
But worry for the poor lost horse,
Sent them on their way.

They crossed a bridge and wandered on,
Down the woodsy trail,
When all of the sudden, on a simple stone,
Sami slipped and fell.

"Awwww, Thomas! I've fallen hard,
And I cannot move an inch,"
Said Sami with a tearful face,
"My ankle feels like it's really pinched."

"It's alright Sami," Thomas said,
"I'll get you out of here.
Stand up now, I'll help you move,
And wipe up all those tears."

Then behind a tree they heard a sound,
Of something moving about.
And wouldn't you know it, ole Pascal,
Had come when he heard Sami crying out.

He knelt down low and nudged Sami,
To get up on his back.
"Do you think he means it?" Sami asked,
"He's really here to help us back?"

"I'm sure he means it," Thomas said,
"You've rode Pascal before.
Just go real slow, I'll help you up."
And so Sami rode once more.

They headed home across the field,
And past the quiet pond.
"I love it here, my brother dear,
From this day and beyond."

"It looks like Pascal saved the day,"
Said Thomas as they walked.
And through the fields they made their way,
While the brother and sister talked.

There at last was the old wood barn,
With their grandma pacing around,
"We did it Grandma!" Sami screamed,
"Just look at who we found."

Thomas helped his sister off Pascal,
And said, "I think she hurt her foot."
"Well, we'd best get it checked," their grandma said,
"But I think the car's kaput."

"It's alright Grandma," Sami said,
"There's a carriage in the stall.
We can hitch it to dear Pascal's back,
And then he can haul us all."

So they hitched the carriage and climbed on board,
And clip-clopped down the lane.
This made Sami so happy,
That she didn't notice any pain.

"This is much too fast!" their Grandma yelled,
As Thomas held the reins.
And with those words he slowed Pascal,
So they ambled past fields of grains.

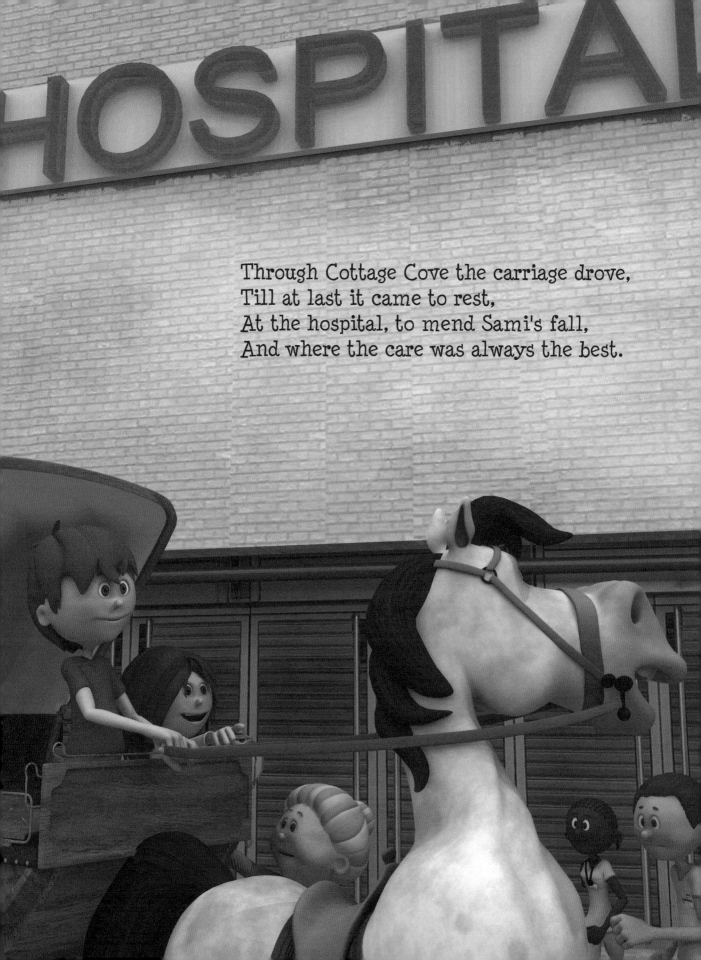

Through Cottage Cove the carriage drove,
Till at last it came to rest,
At the hospital, to mend Sami's fall,
And where the care was always the best.

They were helped inside and tended to,
By a doctor and a nurse.
It was a simple sprain that caused the pain,
But it could have been much worse.

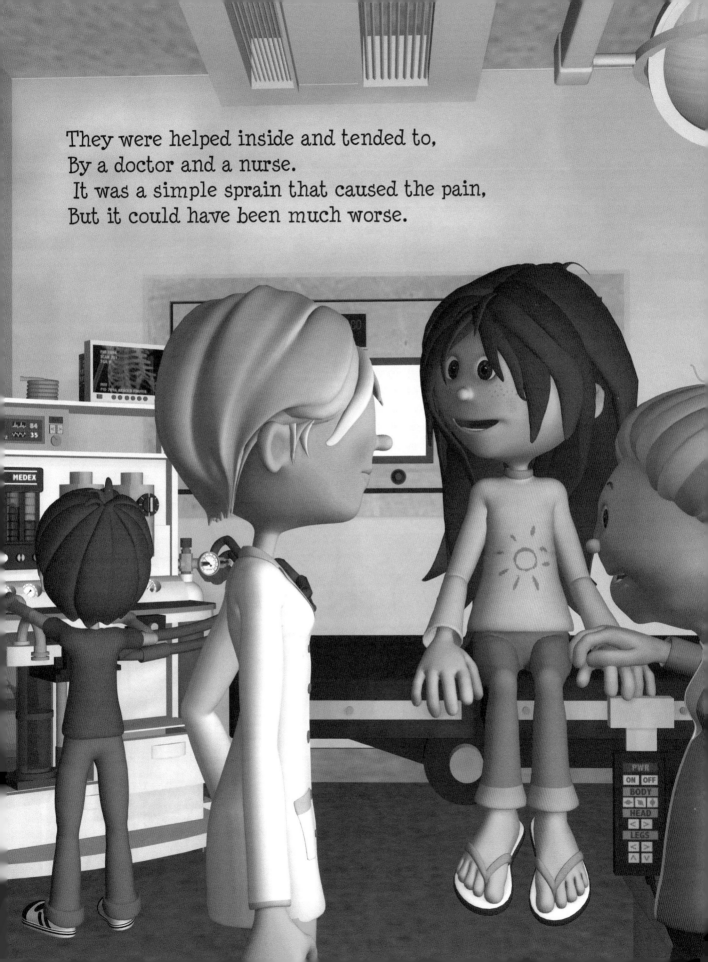

"Let's go on home," said Grandma Lamb.
"I think this day is done."
"I love you Grandma," Sami said,
"For this day of horse-filled fun."

So they climbed aboard and headed home,
Like so many times before,
But it was so much better in a horse and carriage,
A moment Sami would always adore.

They put Pascal back in the barn,
And made sure the gate would stay.
Then Sami Lamb she hugged that horse,
Because she didn't know what else to say.

They went inside to end the night,
And have a bite to eat,
But wouldn't you know it, the kids conked out,
Before the shoes were off their feet.

The morning came and the kids awoke,
To the sound of their mom and dad.
And Henry showed up shortly after,
Which made everybody glad.

"I rode Pascal!" said Sami Lamb,
As she hugged her father's face.
"This has been the best time of my life,
Even better than going to outer space."

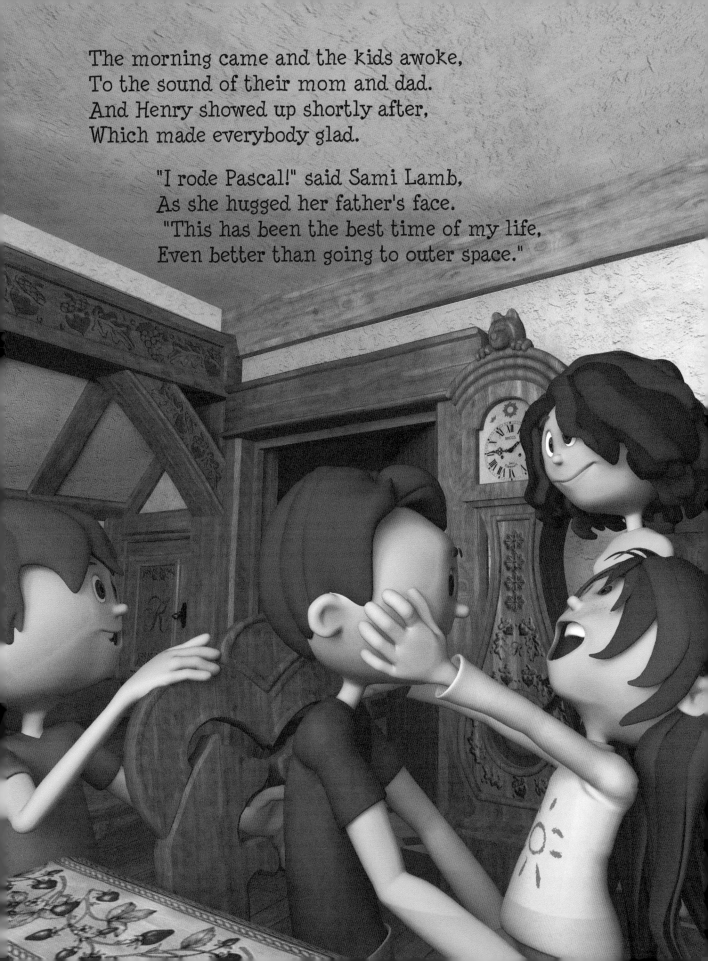

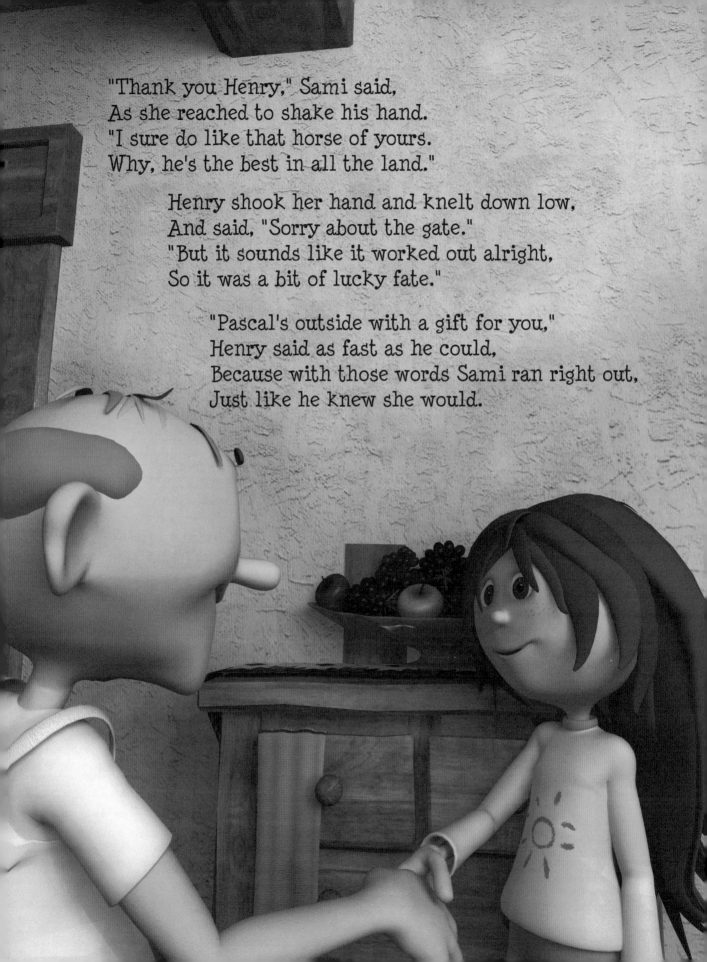

"Thank you Henry," Sami said,
As she reached to shake his hand.
"I sure do like that horse of yours.
Why, he's the best in all the land."

Henry shook her hand and knelt down low,
And said, "Sorry about the gate."
"But it sounds like it worked out alright,
So it was a bit of lucky fate."

"Pascal's outside with a gift for you,"
Henry said as fast as he could,
Because with those words Sami ran right out,
Just like he knew she would.

Sami burst outside and there he was,
With a ribbon round his neck,
And hanging there was a new horseshoe,
As a reminder of their trek.

"I'll be back soon, my dearest friend,"
Said Sami as she cried.
"These tears aren't cause I'm feeling bad,
It's just I hate to say goodbye."

And that right there's how Sami Lamb,
Met Pascal the horse.
And you bet it's true, and we all knew,
That they'd be best friends of course.

The End

Through The Milky Way On A PB&J

James McDonald

Rainy Day Poems

James McDonald

Made in the USA
Lexington, KY
24 August 2014